British Library Cataloguing in Publication Data

100 nursery rhymes.—(Nursery rhymes & stories)
  1. Nursery rhymes, English
  I. McKie, Anne   II. McKie, Ken   III. Series
  398'.8   PZ8.3
  ISBN 0-7214-0965-2

First edition

Published by Ladybird Books Ltd Loughborough Leicestershire UK
Ladybird Books Inc Auburn Maine 04210 USA

© LADYBIRD BOOKS LTD MCMLXXXVI

Printed in England

One hundred
Nursery Rhymes

selected by ANNE McKIE
illustrated by KEN McKIE

Ladybird Books

Girls and boys come out to play, .
The moon doth shine as bright as day;
Come with a whoop and come with a call;
Come with a good will or not at all.

Up the ladder and down the wall,
A halfpenny roll will serve us all;
You find milk and I'll find flour,
And we'll have a pudding in half an hour.

Little Blue Ben, who lives in the glen,
Keeps a blue cat and one blue hen,
Which lays of blue eggs a score and ten;
Where shall I find the little Blue Ben?

A wise old owl sat in an oak,
The more he heard the less he spoke;
The less he spoke the more he heard.
Why aren't we all like that wise bird?

The Lion and the Unicorn
        were fighting for the crown,
The Lion beat the Unicorn
            all round the town.
Some gave them white bread
    and some gave them brown,
And some gave them plum cake
    and drummed them out of town.

Red sky at night,
Shepherd's delight,
Red sky in the morning,
Shepherd's warning.

A diller, a dollar,
A ten o'clock scholar,
What makes you come so soon?
You used to come at ten o'clock,
But now you come at noon.

One misty, moisty morning,
When cloudy was the weather,
There I met an old man
Clothed all in leather.

I took him by the hand,
And told him very plain,
'How do you do? How do you do?
And how do you do again?'

Charley Parley stole the barley
Out of the baker's shop.
The baker came out,
　　　　and gave him a clout,
Which made poor Charley hop.

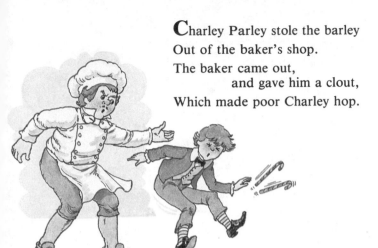

I'll sing you a song,
Though not very long,
Yet I think it as pretty as any.
Put your hand in your purse,
You'll never be worse,
And give the poor singer a penny.

Oh, dear! What can the matter be?
Dear, dear! What can the matter be?
Oh, dear! What can the matter be?
Johnny's so long at the fair.

He promised to buy me
                    a basket of posies,
A garland of lilies, a garland of roses,
A little straw hat
             to set off the blue ribbons,
That tie up my bonny brown hair.

Bye, baby bunting,
Daddy's gone a-hunting,
Gone to get a rabbit skin
To wrap the baby bunting in.

Up and down the City Road,
In and out the Eagle,
That's the way the money goes,
Pop goes the weasel!

Half a pound of tuppenny rice,
Half a pound of treacle,
Mix it up and make it nice,
Pop goes the weasel!

Every night when I go out,
The monkey's on the table;
Take a stick and knock it off,
Pop goes the weasel!

London Bridge is falling down,
Falling down, falling down,
London Bridge is falling down,
My fair lady.

Fee, fi, fo, fum,
I smell the blood of an Englishman:
Be he alive or be he dead,
I'll grind his bones to make my bread.

Cobbler, cobbler mend my shoe,
Get it done by half past two,
Stitch it up and stitch it down
And then I'll give you half a crown.

See a pin and pick it up
All that day you'll have good luck,
See a pin and let it lay
Bad luck you'll have all that day.

Rain on the green grass,
And rain on the tree,
Rain on the house-top,
But not on me.

11

Roses are red,
Violets are blue,
Sugar is sweet
And so are you.

Here we go round the mulberry bush,
The mulberry bush, the mulberry bush,
Here we go round the mulberry bush,
On a cold and frosty morning.

Gregory Griggs, Gregory Griggs,
Had twenty-seven different wigs,
He wore them up, he wore them down,
To please the people of the town;
He wore them east, he wore them west,
But he never could tell which he
loved the best.

Riddle me, riddle me ree,
A little man in a tree;
A stick in his hand,
A stone in his throat,
If you read me this riddle
I'll give you a groat.

MARKET

To market, to market,
To buy a plum bun;
Home again, home again,
Market is done.

As Tommy Snooks and Bessy Brooks
Were walking out on Sunday,
Says Tommy Snooks to Bessy Brooks,
Tomorrow will be Monday.

Charley Barley, butter and eggs,
Sold his wife for three duck eggs.
When the ducks began to lay
Charley Barley flew away.

It's raining, it's pouring,
The old man's snoring;
He went to bed
And bumped his head
And couldn't get up
      in the morning.

Cuckoo, cuckoo, what do you do?
In April I open my bill;
In May I sing all the day;
In June I change my tune;
In July away I fly;
In August away I must.

A-hunting we will go!
A-hunting we will go!
We'll catch a fox,
And put him in a box.
A-hunting we will go!

Here we go Looby Loo,
Here we go Looby Light,
Here we go Looby Loo,
All on a Saturday night.
I put my right hand in,
I put my right hand out,
I give my right hand a shake,
Shake, shake
And turn myself about.

Monday's child is fair of face,
Tuesday's child is full of grace,
Wednesday's child is full of woe,
Thursday's child has far to go,
Friday's child is loving and giving,
Saturday's child works hard for its living,
But the child that's born on the Sabbath day
Is bonny and blithe, and good and gay.

Dance to your daddy,
My little laddie,
Dance to your daddy,
My little lamb.

You shall have a fishy
In a little dishy,
You shall have a fishy
When the boat comes in.

'Fire! Fire!' said Mrs Dyer;
'Where? Where?' said Mrs Dare;
'Up the town,' said Mrs Brown;
'Any damage?' said Mrs Gamage;
'None at all,' said Mrs Hall.

Tweedledum and Tweedledee
Agreed to have a battle,
For Tweedledum said Tweedledee
Had spoiled his nice new rattle.
Just then flew by a monstrous crow
As black as a tar-barrel,
Which frightened both the heroes so,
They quite forgot their quarrel.

Incy Wincy spider
Climbing up the spout;
Down came the rain
And washed the spider out.
Out came the sunshine
And dried up all the rain;
Incy Wincy spider
Climbed up the spout again.

Round and round the rugged rock
The ragged rascal ran.

This old man, he played one,
He played Nick Nack
On my drum!
Nick Nack Paddy Whack!
Give a dog a bone,
This old man came rolling home.

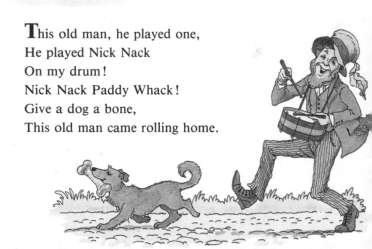

Upon Paul's steeple stands a tree.
As full of apples as may be,
The little boys of London town,
They run with hooks to pull them down.
And then they run from hedge to hedge
Until they come to London Bridge.

The man in the wilderness asked of me,
'How many strawberries grew in the sea?'
I answered him, as I thought good,
'As many red herrings
As grew in the wood.'

As I was going to St Ives,
I met a man with seven wives,
Each wife had seven sacks;
Each sack had seven cats;
Each cat had seven kittens.
Kits, cats, sacks, and wives,
How many were going to St Ives?

Star light, star bright,
First star I see tonight.
I wish I may, I wish I might
Have the wish I wish tonight.

Into the basin, put in the plums,
Stir – about, stir – about, stir – about!

Next the good white flour comes,
Stir – about, stir – about, stir – about!

Sugar and peel and eggs and spice,
Stir – about, stir – about, stir – about!

Mix them and fix them
         and cook them twice,
Stir – about, stir – about, stir – about!

Please to remember
The fifth of November,
Gunpowder, treason and plot;
I see no reason
Why gunpowder treason
Should ever be forgot.

If wishes were horses,
        beggars would ride.
If turnips were watches,
      I'd wear one by my side,
If 'ifs' and 'ands'
        were pots and pans,
There'd be no work for tinkers.

'**O**ranges and lemons,'
Say the bells of St Clement's.

'You owe me five farthings,'
Say the bells of St Martin's.

'When will you pay me?'
Say the bells at Old Bailey.

'When I grow rich,'
Say the bells at Shoreditch.

'Pray, when will that be?'
Say the bells at Stepney.

'I'm sure I don't know,'
Says the great bell at Bow.

Here comes a candle
To light you to bed,
Here comes a chopper
To chop off your head.

Tinker, Tailor, Soldier, Sailor,
Richman, Poorman, Beggarman, Thief,
Lady, Baby, Gypsy, Queen.

Betty Botter bought some butter,
'But,' she said, 'the butter's bitter;
If I put it in my batter
It will make my batter bitter,
But a bit of better butter,
That would make my batter better.'
So she bought a bit of butter
Better than her bitter butter,
And she put it in her batter.
And the batter was not bitter.
So 'twas better Betty Botter
Bought a bit of better butter.

One for sorrow, two for joy,
Three for a girl, four for a boy,
Five for silver, six for gold,
Seven for a secret ne'er to be told.

Solomon Grundy,
Born on a Monday,
Christened on Tuesday,
Married on Wednesday,
Took ill on Thursday,
Worse on Friday,
Died on Saturday,
Buried on Sunday,
This is the end
Of Solomon Grundy.

Jerry Hall
He is so small
A rat could eat him,
Hat and all.

She sells seashells on the seashore;
The shells that she sells are seashells I'm sure.
So if she sells seashells on the seashore,
I'm sure that the shells are seashore shells.

Rain, rain, go away,
Come again another day.

Up the wooden hill
To Bedfordshire,
Down Sheet Lane
To Blanket Fair.

Peter Piper picked a peck
              of pickled pepper;
A peck of pickled pepper
              Peter Piper picked.
If Peter Piper picked a peck
              of pickled pepper,
Where's the peck of pickled pepper
              Peter Piper picked?

Two legs sat upon three legs
With one leg in his lap.
In comes four legs
And runs away with one leg.
Up jumps two legs,
Picks up three legs,
Throws it after four legs,
And makes him bring one leg back.

Christmas is coming,
The geese are getting fat,
Please put a penny
In the old man's hat.
If you haven't got a penny,
A ha'penny will do;
If you haven't got a ha'penny,
Then God bless you!

Three wise men of Gotham
They went to sea in a bowl;
If the bowl had been stronger,
My song had been longer.

All work and no play
makes Jack a dull boy;

All play and no work
makes Jack a mere toy.

I see the moon,
And the moon sees me;
God bless the moon,
And God bless me.

Heeper-peeper, chimney sweeper,
Had a wife and couldn't keep her.
Had another, didn't love her,
Up the chimney he did shove her.

Six little mice sat down to spin;
Pussy passed by and she peeped in,
'What are you doing, my little men?'
'Weaving coats for gentlemen.'
'Shall I come in
            and cut off your threads?'
'No, no, Mistress Pussy,
            you'll bite off our heads.'
'Oh no, I'll not; I'll help you to spin.'
'That may be so,
            but you don't come in.'

Punch and Judy
Fought for a pie;
Punch gave Judy
A knock in the eye.

Says Punch to Judy,
'Will you have any more?'
Says Judy to Punch,
'My eye is too sore.'

Thirty days hath September,
April, June and November;
All the rest have thirty-one,
Excepting February alone,
And that has twenty-eight days clear
And twenty-nine in each leap year.

A cat came fiddling out of a barn,
With a pair of bagpipes under her arm;
She could sing nothing but fiddle-cum-fee,
The mouse has married the bumblebee.
Pipe, cat; dance, mouse,
We'll have a wedding at our good house.

I'll tell you a story of Jack-a-Nory,
And now my story's begun,
I'll tell you another of Jack and his brother,
And now my story's done.

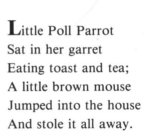

Little Poll Parrot
Sat in her garret
Eating toast and tea;
A little brown mouse
Jumped into the house
And stole it all away.

I shot an arrow in the air,
It fell to earth, I know not where.

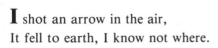

If all the world were paper,
And all the sea were ink,
And all the trees were bread and cheese,
What should we have to drink?

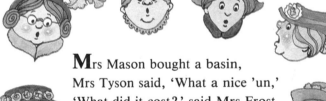

Mrs Mason bought a basin,
Mrs Tyson said, 'What a nice 'un,'
'What did it cost?' said Mrs Frost,
'Half a crown,' said Mrs Brown,
'Did it indeed,' said Mrs Reed,
'It did for certain,' said Mrs Burton.
Then Mrs Nix, up to her tricks
Threw the basin on the bricks.

One, two,
Buckle my shoe;

Three, four,
Knock at the door;

Five, six,
Pick up sticks;

Seven, eight,
Lay them straight;

Nine, ten,
A big fat hen.

Ring a ring o' roses,
A pocket full of posies.
A-tishoo! A-tishoo!
We all fall down.

How many miles to Babylon?
Three score miles and ten.
Can I get there by candlelight?
Aye, and back again.

Snail, snail,
        put out your horns,
And I'll give you bread
        and barley corns.

Shoe the horse, shoe the horse.
Shoe the bay mare.
Here a nail, there a nail,
Still, she stands there.

Lavender's blue, diddle-diddle,
Rosemary's green,
When I am king, diddle-diddle,
You shall be queen.

Twinkle, twinkle, little star,
How I wonder what you are!
Up above the world so high,
Like a diamond in the sky.

Hark, hark, the dogs do bark,
The beggars are coming to town.
Some in rags, and some in tags,
And one in a velvet gown.

There was a bee, sat on a wall,
It said, 'Buzz, buzz.'
And that was all.

Jingle bells, jingle bells,
Jingle all the way.

O what fun it is to ride,
In a one-horse open sleigh.

Little Nancy Etticoat
In a white petticoat,
The longer she stands
The shorter she grows.

Ladybird, ladybird, fly away home,
Your house is on fire and your children all gone;
All but one, and her name is Ann,
And she crept under the frying pan.

'Come, let's to bed,'
Says Sleepy-Head;
'Tarry a while,' says Slow;
'Put on the pan,'
Says Greedy-Nan,
'Let's sup before we go.'

Rock-a-bye baby,
Thy cradle is green,
Father's a nobleman,
Mother's a queen.
Johnny's a drummer
And drums for the King.
And Betty's a lady,
And wears a gold ring.

'Pretty maid, pretty maid,
Where have you been?'
'Gathering a posy,
To give to the Queen.'

'Pretty maid, pretty maid,
What gave she you?'
'She gave me a diamond
As big as my shoe.'

Jeremiah, blow the fire,
Puff, puff, puff!
First you blow it gently,
Then you blow it rough.

Dame Trot and her cat
Sat down for a chat;
The Dame sat on this side
And puss sat on that.

'Puss,' says the Dame,
'Can you catch a rat,
Or a mouse in the dark?'
'Purr,' says the cat.

Daffy-down-dilly is now
        come to town,
With a yellow petticoat,
        and a green gown.

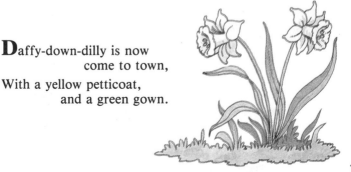

37

Hush, little baby, don't say a word,
Papa's going to buy you a mocking bird.

If the mocking bird won't sing,
Papa's going to buy you a diamond ring.

If the diamond ring turns to brass,
Papa's going to buy you a looking-glass.

If the looking-glass gets broke,
Papa's going to buy you a billy-goat.

If that billy-goat runs away,
Papa's going to buy you another today.

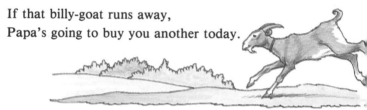

Little fishes in a brook,
Father caught them on a hook,
Mother fried them in a pan,
Johnnie eats them like a man.

My mother said I never should
Play with the gypsies in the wood.
If I did, she would say:
'Naughty little girl to disobey.'

Go to bed late,
Stay very small;
Go to bed early,
Grow very tall.

Young lambs to sell,
young lambs to sell,
If I'd as much money
as I could tell,
I wouldn't be crying,
'Young lambs to sell.'

Go to bed first,
A golden purse;
Go to bed second,
A golden pheasant;
Go to bed third,
A golden bird.

Sally go round the sun,
Sally go round the moon,
Sally go round the chimney-pots,
On a Saturday afternoon.

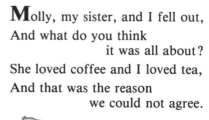

Molly, my sister, and I fell out,
And what do you think
                it was all about?
She loved coffee and I loved tea,
And that was the reason
                we could not agree.

40

The Man in the moon
        came tumbling down,
To ask his way to Norwich.
He went by the south
        and burnt his mouth,
By eating cold plum-porridge.

Cross-patch, draw the latch,
Sit by the fire and spin,
Take a cup and drink it up,
Then call your neighbours in.

Blow, wind, blow! And go, mill, go!
That the miller may grind his corn;
That the baker may take it,
And into bread make it.
And bring us a loaf in the morn.

Barber, barber, shave a pig
How many hairs to make a wig?
Four and twenty, that's enough,
Give the barber a pinch of snuff.

Old Farmer Giles,
Walked seven miles
With his faithful dog, old Rover;
And old Farmer Giles,
When he came to the stiles,
Took a run, and jumped clean over.

The man in the moon looked out of the moon,
Looked out of the moon and said,
''Tis time for all children on the earth
To think about getting to bed!'

Good night,
Sleep tight,
Wake up bright
In the morning light,
To do what's right.
With all your might.